Gretchen Groundhog,
It's Your Day!

Abby Levine

ILLUSTRATIONS BY **Nancy Cote**

SCHOLASTIC INC.

New York Toronto London Auckland Sydney
Mexico City New Delhi Hong Kong

For Lynn: May the
winters be short.
A. L.

To Katie, whose sense
of joy, sensitivity, and
compassion keep me
aspiring to become the
best that I can be.
Love ya, Mom.
N. C.

ISBN 0-439-18815-6

Copyright © 1998 by Abby Levine.
Illustrations copyright © 1998 by Nancy Cote.
All rights reserved.
Published by Scholastic Inc., 555 Broadway, New York, NY 10012,
by arrangement with Albert Whitman & Company.
SCHOLASTIC and associated logos are trademarks and/or registered
trademarks of Scholastic Inc.

15 14 13   5 6/0

Printed in the U.S.A.   40

First Scholastic printing, January 2001

The illustrations were done in watercolor, pencil, and gouache.
The design is by Scott Piehl.

About Groundhog Day

If Candlemas is fair and clear, there'll be two winters in the year.

The groundhog, also called a woodchuck or marmot, is a roundish furry animal about the size of a big cat. It is actually a kind of squirrel that lives in the ground. Groundhogs can be found in many areas of the United States, though they're most common in the East. They hibernate in the winter.

In medieval times, people believed that all hibernating animals emerged on Candlemas. This Christian festival falls on February 2 and is the day when farmers in northern Europe traditionally have started their spring planting. If the day was sunny and animals saw their shadows, they would return to their dens to sleep, and winter would continue for six more weeks. If the day was cloudy, then spring would soon arrive. German pioneers in Pennsylvania transferred this belief to the groundhog.

Groundhog Day is celebrated in many American towns. The custom began on February 2, 1887, when people in Punxsutawney, Pennsylvania, hiked to the burrow of a groundhog named Phil and watched him give his first forecast. Since then, Punxsutawney Phil and his yearly weather predictions on Groundhog Day have become famous all over the world.

It was a dark and snowy night. Gretchen Groundhog sat in her burrow, worrying. In a few days it would be February 2, when the world would be watching the little town of Piccadilly.

On that day, for the first time, Gretchen would step from her burrow to stand before TV cameras, newspaper reporters, tourists, all the townsfolk, and a brass band. Everyone would be waiting as Gretchen looked for her shadow.

For as long as she could remember, it had been Great-Uncle Gus who searched for his shadow before the anxious crowd.

If he saw it, there would be a roar of disappointment, for this meant winter would last six more dreary weeks. The band would play slow, sad music, and Gus would trudge back into his burrow.

If there was no shadow, the band would play a lively tune, and everyone would hug and cheer. Spring was around the corner!

But now Great-Uncle Gus was too old.
It was up to Gretchen, his only relative, to carry on.
    "I can't do it," Gretchen told her great-uncle.
"I'm just too shy. I can't stand there with
everyone looking at me."
    "You can do it," said Great-Uncle Gus.
"The first time is always the hardest."
    But Gretchen knew she could
not Go Out.

"Gretchen's not Going Out!" The news flashed through Piccadilly. "What will we do?" the townsfolk asked each other.

On January 30, there was a story about Gretchen on the front page of the *Post*.

"PICCADILLY PUZZLED"

the headline said. The story continued, "There has always been a Groundhog Day in Piccadilly. But this year, it seems Gretchen Groundhog will not Go Out. How will we plan if we do not know when winter will end?"

The townsfolk stopped Gretchen on the street. They peppered her with questions.

"Should we buy more salt to put on icy roads?" asked the mayor.

A father asked, "Shall I chop more wood for my family?"

"When can the bears stop hibernating?" asked a little boy.

"Please," everyone begged. "Please, dear Gretchen, Go Out on Groundhog Day. Tell us when winter will end!"

But Gretchen only shook her head.

On January 31, Gretchen lit a cheery fire, but it did not help her mood. All day the doorbell chimed, the phone rang, e-mail erupted, and urgent letters plopped through the mail slot. Gretchen felt terrible. It seemed like the longest day of her life.

On February 1, the town was in an uproar. Tourists filled the motels. In front of Gretchen's burrow, carpenters were building wooden stands for the crowd. The TV crews had arrived, and the band was practicing with squawky sounds. Groundhog Day was only hours away!

"PICCADILLY PANICKED"

read the *Post*. "Soon the eyes of the world will be upon us. What will happen if Gretchen does not Go Out?"

KNOCK! KNOCK! KNOCK!

Three townsfolk were waiting when Gretchen opened her door.

"You *must* try, Gretchen," said the town historian. "There has always been a Groundhog Day in Piccadilly."

"Do, Gretchen. I'll stand beside you," said the chief of police.

"I'll make you famous," said the editor of the *Post*.

But Gretchen only shook her head.

All afternoon and evening, visitors came.
KNOCK! KNOCK! KNOCK! "Gretchen, are you there?"
KNOCK! KNOCK! KNOCK! "Gretchen!"

That night, weary and sad, Gretchen fell asleep in her
rocking chair. But she heard the townsfolk even in her dreams.
KNOCK! KNOCK! KNOCK! "Please, Gretchen, open
the door!"

Gretchen awoke, but the knocking did not stop. She hurried
to the door and looked out the peephole. There, on the moonlit
snow, stood a little girl. It was Hester, the town historian's
daughter.

"May I come in?" Hester asked.

Gretchen opened the door.

She helped Hester take off her coat, soggy mittens, and wet boots and muffler.

"I won't stay long," Hester said. "I wanted you to see these. I found them while I was helping my mother."

She held out a wooden box with some yellowed pieces of paper in it. Gretchen could see that they had old-fashioned writing on them.

"What's this?" Gretchen asked.

"Records from our town history," Hester explained.

While Great-Uncle Gus made cups of steaming cocoa, Gretchen studied the first piece of paper.

"Tomorrow I Must Go Out," it read, "to Stand Before the Pilgrims and the Indians. I Am Greatly Afeared." It was signed "Goody Groundhog."

Gretchen was amazed. "Goody Groundhog lived a long time ago! She came to America on the *Mayflower*, before there was a Piccadilly."

"My mother says Goody told everyone the Second Winter would be better than the First," said Hester. "They were very glad."

Gretchen leafed through the papers. "Here's one by George Groundhog at Valley Forge!" she exclaimed. "He says, 'I Am Affrighted to Go Out, but I Shall. The Winter Has Been Long and Hard. The Soldiers Must Know What Will Be.'"

"My mother says George told them the winter would go on a long time," said Hester. "Everyone was very sad."

George Groundhog

General Grant Groundhog

Gene GroundHog

Gloria G.

As Gretchen read through the papers, she became more and more excited. There was a page from brave General Grant Groundhog, who had fought in the Civil War. And Gene Groundhog, the tough cowboy. And Gloria Groundhog, who became a movie star.

"They were all afraid to Go Out!" Gretchen said.

She read the last piece of paper. "I am scared, but tomorrow
I will try to Go Out," it said. It was signed "Gus Groundhog."
"You?" said Gretchen to Great-Uncle Gus.

Her great-uncle looked surprised. Then a dreamy look came into his eyes. "It was so long ago I had forgotten it," he said. "Now I remember—I couldn't eat or sleep the night before."

"What happened then?" asked Gretchen.

"My great-uncle Grover helped me," said Gus. "He said, 'You can do it, Gus. The first time is always the hardest.'"

The clock began to chime. "...nine, ten, eleven, twelve," they counted together. "Oh, my gosh, I've got to go!" Hester said. "I've never stayed up so late!"

"Thank you for everything, Hester," Gretchen said. She and Hester gave each other a big hug.

Gretchen went to bed and lay quietly in the darkness. She thought about the next morning, about all the townsfolk gathered, the TV cameras and the crowds, the blaring of the band. She turned on the light, wrote a few lines on a piece of paper, and put it in the history box. Then she closed her eyes and fell asleep.

Gretchen's dreams were peaceful. She was awoken by the sound of voices and the screeks of the band tuning up.

She put on her coat and muffler, boots and mittens. She took a deep breath. "You can do it," she whispered to herself. Then Gretchen Groundhog flung open the door...

and stepped out into the February morning.